Care Bears™

Official Handbook

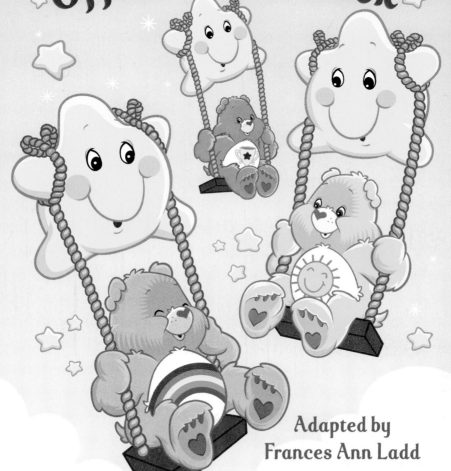

Adapted by
Frances Ann Ladd

SCHOLASTIC INC.

New York Toronto London Auckland Sydney
Mexico City New Delhi Hong Kong Buenos Aires

Interior Designed by Amy Heinrich

ISBN 0-439-66402-0

Published by Scholastic Inc.

12 11 10 9 8 7 6 5 4 3 2 1 4 5 6 7 8/0

Printed in the U.S.A.
First printing, August 2004

Care Bears™

Welcome to the Care Bears Official Handbook!

Here you'll find everything you ever wanted to know about the Care Bears—the caringest, sharingest, furriest friends around! You'll even meet the Care Bear Cousins—wonderful friends who live among the cloud-trees in the Forest of Feelings. The Care Bears know everyone is full of feelings—from silly to sad, grumpy to glad, and everything in between. Each Care Bear has his or her own special feeling—they even wear their feelings right on their tummies! Maybe you need a little help figuring out your own feelings. The Care Bears are here to help! And most of all, the Care Bears are here to share feelings, friendship, and FUN!

So turn the page, and meet the Care Bears!

What is this wonderful place?

It's a star-speckled, rainbow-trimmed, cotton candy world called Care-a-lot, and it's the home of the Care Bears!

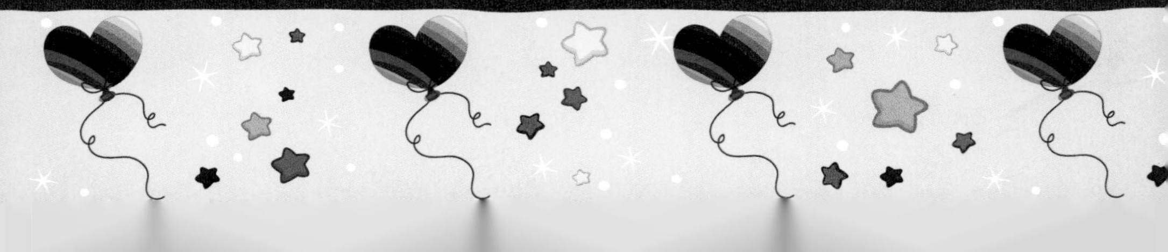

Where is Care-a-lot?

It's here. It's there. It's everywhere there are hearts that love and those who care!

In the heart of Care-a-lot is the Care-a-lot Castle, where the Care Bears gather to help others. Inside the Care-a-lot Castle is the beautiful Hall of the Heart, where the Care Bears meet around a heart-shaped table.

Have you ever heard of the legend of King Arthur and the Knights of the Round Table? The name Care-a-lot sounds a lot like Camelot, King Arthur's wonderful castle. The Care Bears all meet in Care-a-lot Castle around a table; not a round table as in the Arthur legends, but a heart-shaped table. And like the Knights of the Round Table, the Care Bears set off from their castle to share their feelings and show they care.

BEDTIME BEAR

Boy

Color: Blue

Symbol: Moon

Character Summary:
He stays awake so you can sleep!

Sweet dreams! As the Care Bear who helps kids rest, Bedtime Bear is brave, loyal, and can calm all your fears and worries. But when off duty during the day, he sometimes gets confused—dozing off and stumbling into funny situations. But never fear—at night and naptimes, he's always wide awake. He can even see in the dark!

Captain of the Dream Team

With Bedtime Bear around, you're cruisin' for some snoozin'!

Bedtime Bear's best friend is Wish Bear—maybe because dreams and wishes go hand in hand!

Bed bug!

Cheer BEAR

Girl

Color: Pink

Symbol: Rainbow

Character Summary:
The ultimate smile-maker
"Smile when you call me
Cheer Bear!"

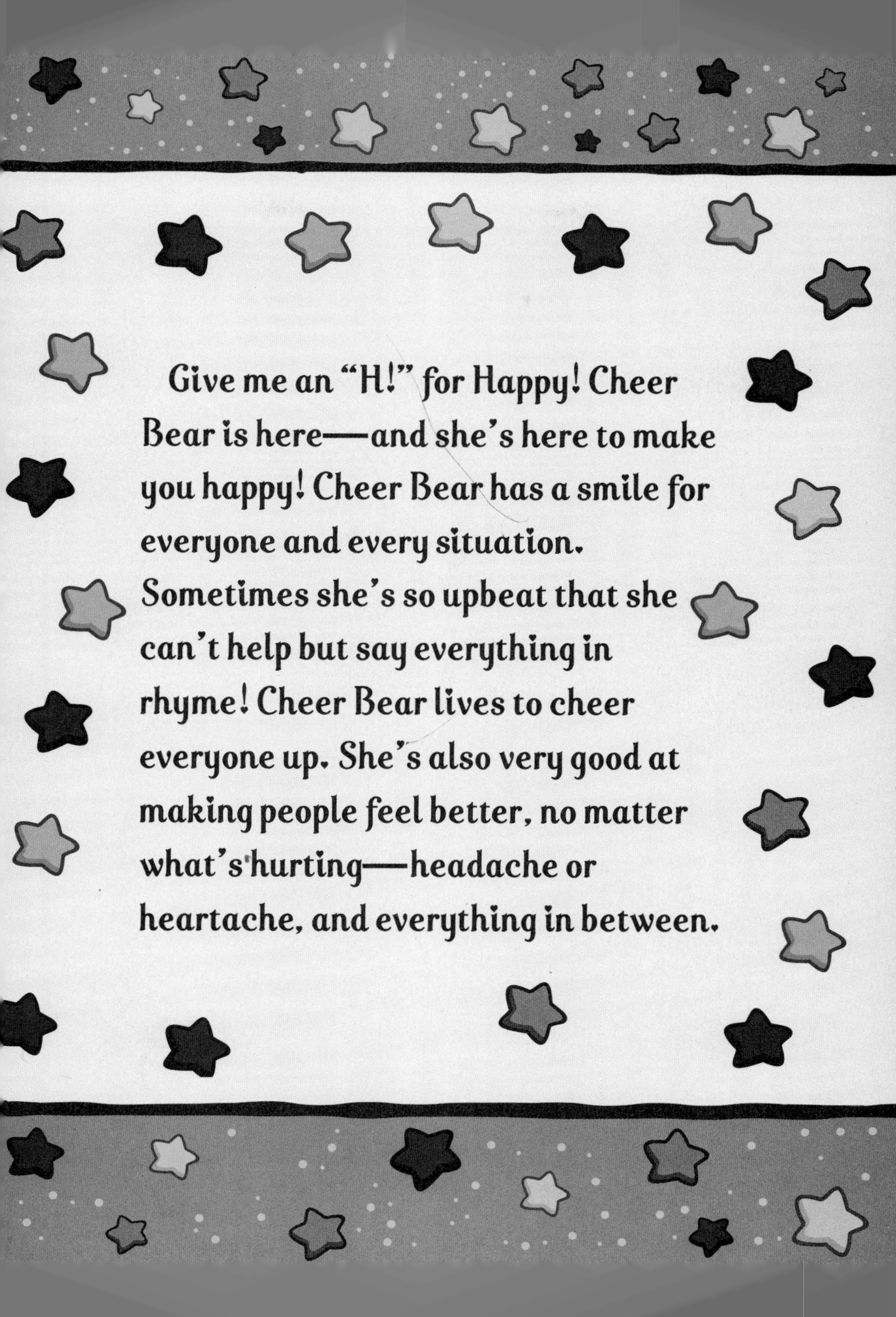

Give me an "H!" for Happy! Cheer Bear is here—and she's here to make you happy! Cheer Bear has a smile for everyone and every situation. Sometimes she's so upbeat that she can't help but say everything in rhyme! Cheer Bear lives to cheer everyone up. She's also very good at making people feel better, no matter what's hurting—headache or heartache, and everything in between.

Cheer Angel!

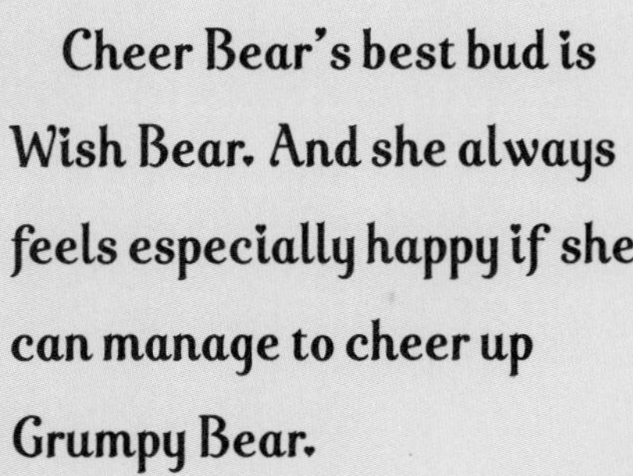

Cheer Bear's best bud is Wish Bear. And she always feels especially happy if she can manage to cheer up Grumpy Bear.

Don't forget, make happiness happen!

Cheerific!

FUNSHINE BEAR

Boy

Color: Yellow

Symbol: Smiling sun

Character Summary:
Class Clown!
King of Fun!

Do you know a class clown? Funshine Bear is the class clown of Care-a-lot! This playful bear knows all the best games to play, and he loves to tell jokes and make funny noises. Even when a day seems gloomy, Funshine Bear helps everyone remember how important it is to laugh and have fun!

Funtastic!

Funshine Bear's best friend is Tenderheart Bear. He gives him good, caring advice when Funshine Bear takes his humor a little too far and doesn't know when "it isn't funny anymore." Share Bear is another special friend. Funshine Bear teases Share Bear instead of telling her he really likes her.

Remember what Funshine Bear always says, "Any time is fun time!"

Shine on!

CHAMP CARE BEAR

Boy

Color: Blue

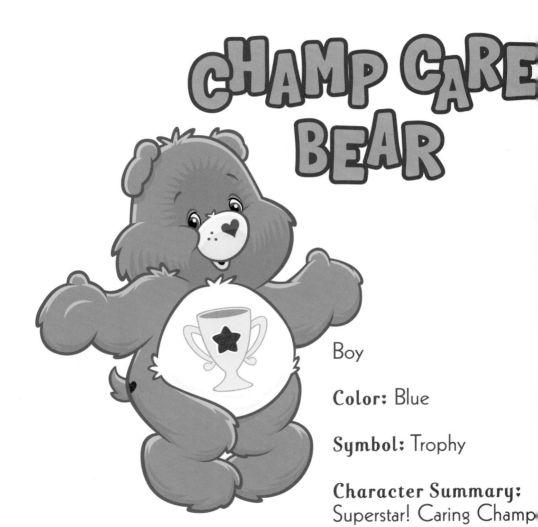

Symbol: Trophy

Character Summary:
Superstar! Caring Champ

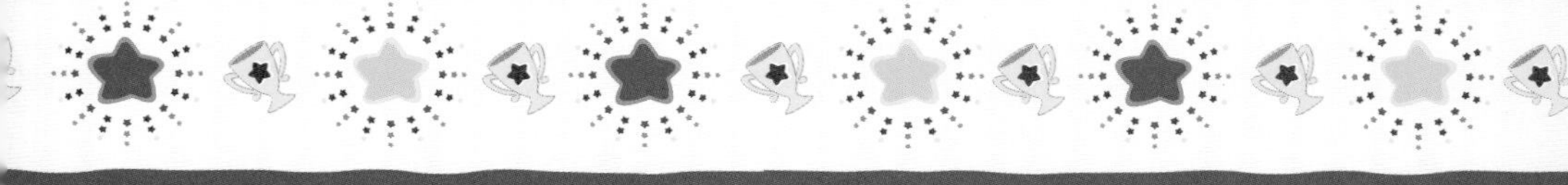

Way to go, Champ Care Bear! He's great at every sport, and can almost make a ball do magic! But Champ's even better at sharing the real prizes of sports—fun, fitness, friendship, and doing your very best!

MVB
Most Valuable Bear

Champ Care Bear's a real team player; he gets along with everybody. But his best bud is Good Luck Bear.

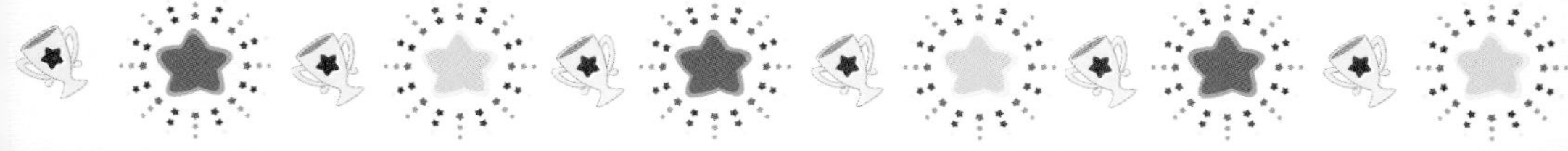

Remember Champ's # 1 saying,
"Give your best to be your best!"

Feeling like a winner!

Share Bear

Girl

Color: Lavender

Symbol: Twin lollipops

Character Summary: Nobody knows how to share like Share Bear. "I do my share of sharing!"

Sharing isn't always easy. But Share Bear loves to share! She even collects little things so she'll always have something to give away. Share Bear knows just how to help kids play well together. Wouldn't you like to have Share Bear at your next playdate?

Share Bear's best pal is Tenderheart Bear. She likes Funshine Bear, too, but he plays too many jokes on her!

Sharing is Caring!

Join the share force!

Share Bear likes to say, "Share a smile! Someone may need one!"

WISH BEAR

Girl

Color: Aqua

Symbol: Shooting Star

Character Summary:
She can make wishes come true—sometimes! Feeling wishful!

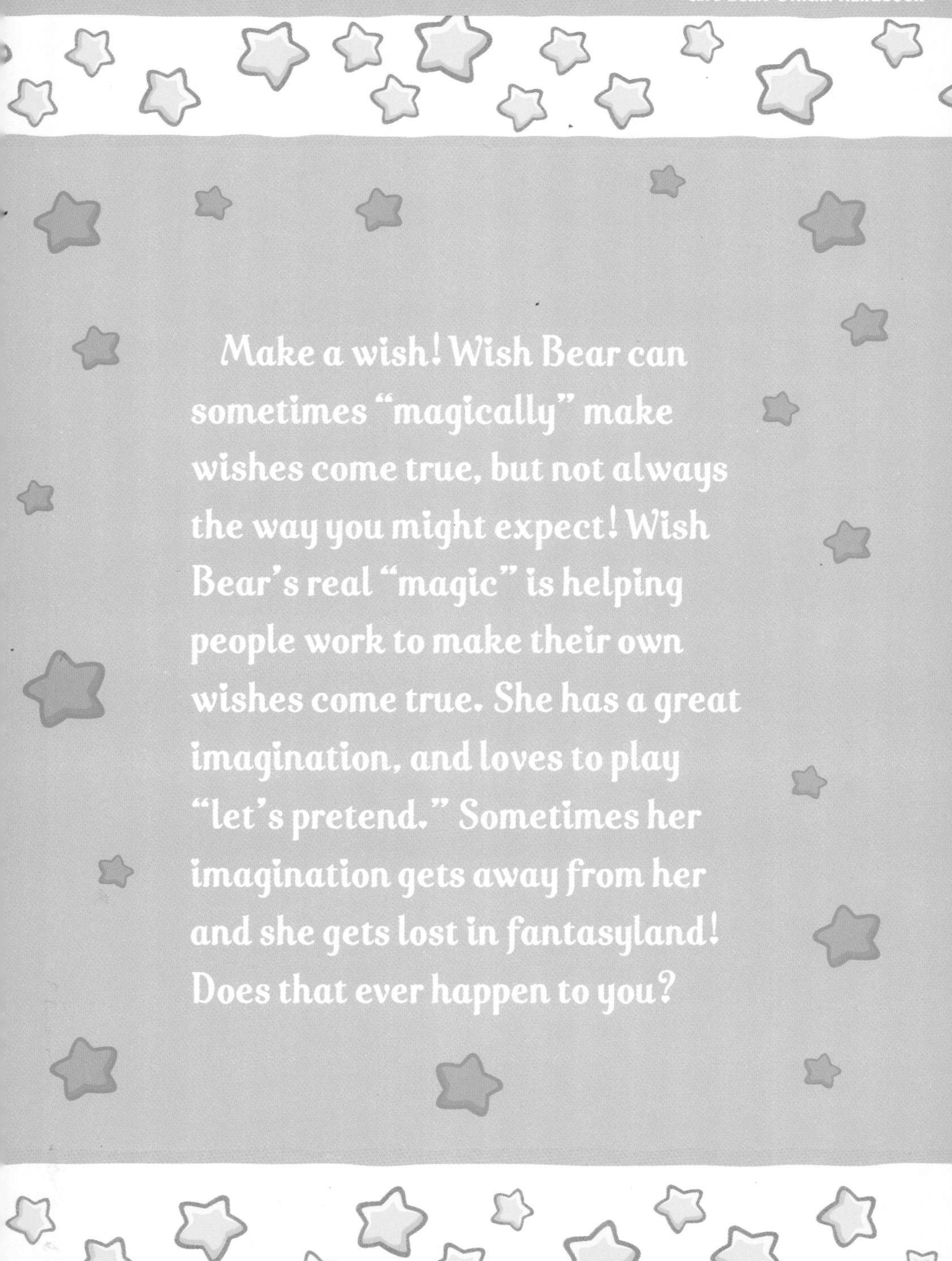

Make a wish! Wish Bear can sometimes "magically" make wishes come true, but not always the way you might expect! Wish Bear's real "magic" is helping people work to make their own wishes come true. She has a great imagination, and loves to play "let's pretend." Sometimes her imagination gets away from her and she gets lost in fantasyland! Does that ever happen to you?

President of the Wishing Star Club!

Wish Bear's special friend is Cheer Bear. Sometimes Wish Bear helps Bedtime Bear with the "night shift."

No matter what, always hold on to your wishes, hopes, and dreams!

Gone wishing

Love-a-lot Bear

Girl

Color: Pink

Symbol: Two hearts

Character Summary:
In love with love.
"I'm all about love!"

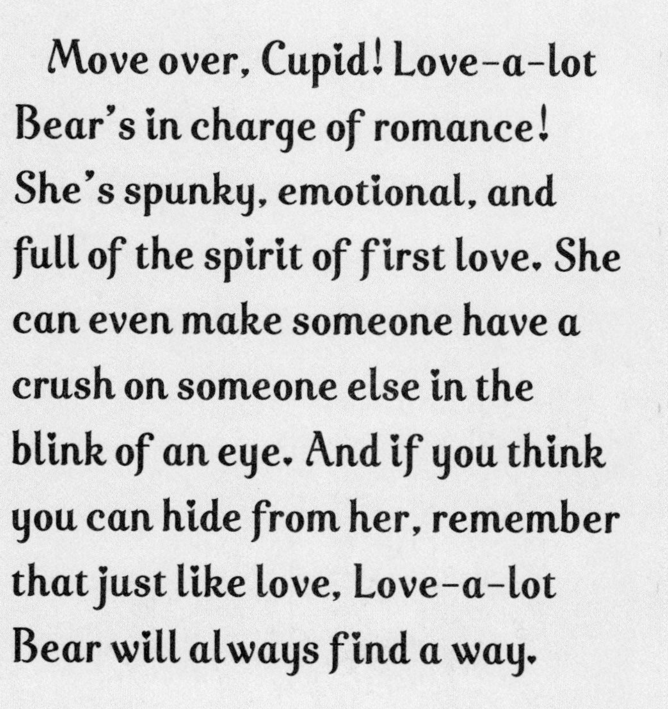

Move over, Cupid! Love-a-lot Bear's in charge of romance! She's spunky, emotional, and full of the spirit of first love. She can even make someone have a crush on someone else in the blink of an eye. And if you think you can hide from her, remember that just like love, Love-a-lot Bear will always find a way.

Lovely

Love-a-lot Bear and Friend Bear are best pals. But she and Good Luck Bear sometimes squabble.

With this lovable little bear,
love is ALWAYS in the air!

All heart

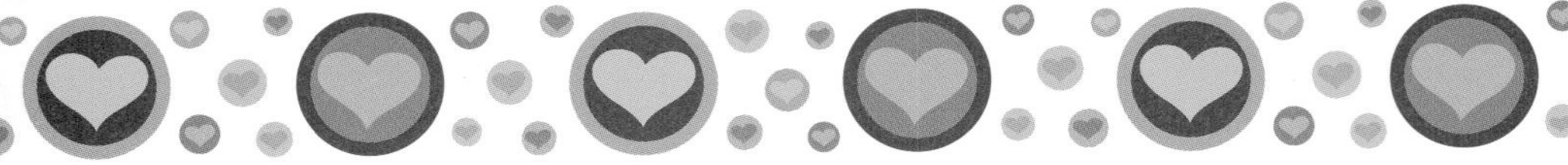

TENDERHEART BEAR

Boy

Color: Brown

Symbol: Heart

Character Summary: The caring-est bear in town! This Bear Cares!

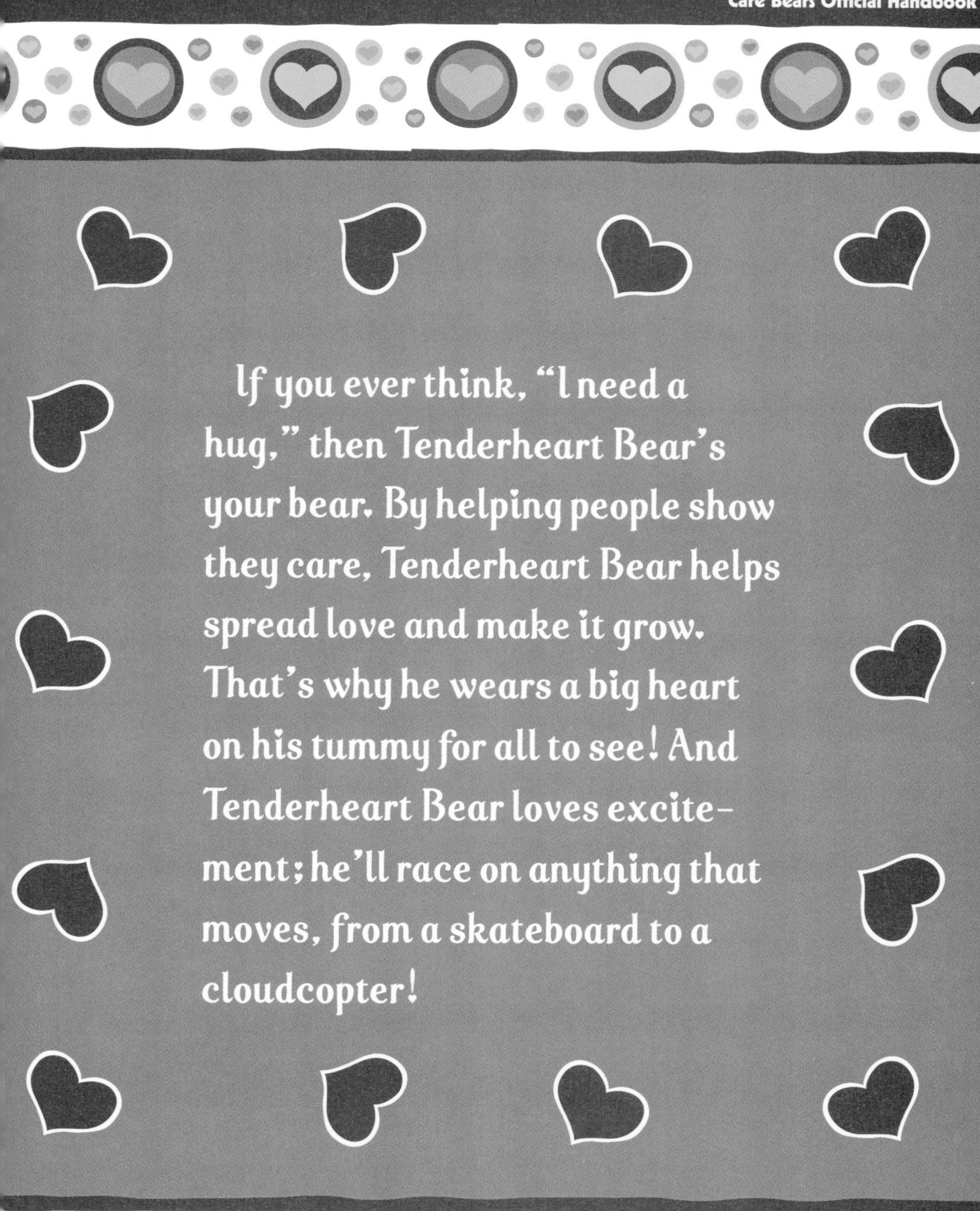

If you ever think, "I need a hug," then Tenderheart Bear's your bear. By helping people show they care, Tenderheart Bear helps spread love and make it grow. That's why he wears a big heart on his tummy for all to see! And Tenderheart Bear loves excitement; he'll race on anything that moves, from a skateboard to a cloudcopter!

King of cuddles!

Tenderheart Bear is usually the leader of all the Care Bears, but he's a special teacher to Cheer Bear and Funshine Bear. His best friends are Share Bear and Grumpy Bear.

Always remember to dare to care!

Feeling big-hearted

GRUMPY BEAR

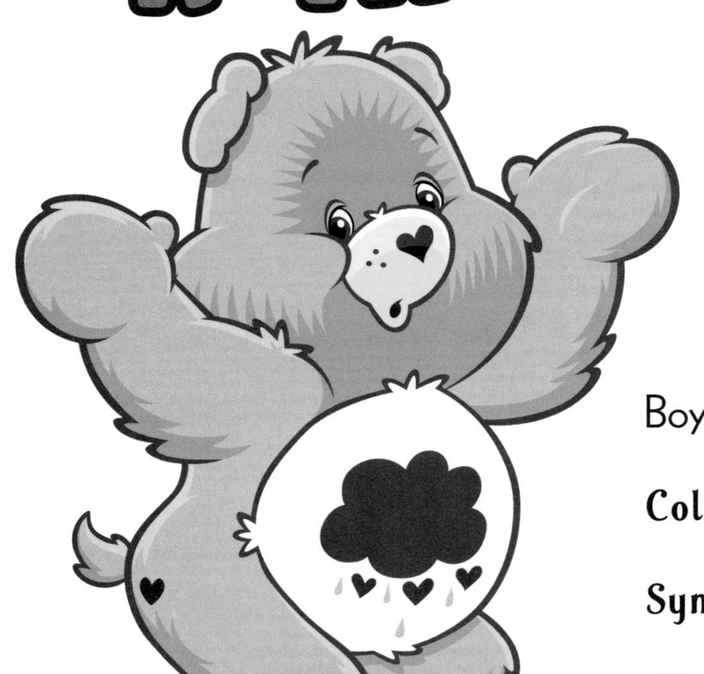

Boy

Color: Blue

Symbol: Rain cloud

Character Summary:
Lovable Grump.
"Who are you calling Grumpy?"

Grumpy Bear shows that it's okay to be in a bad mood sometimes. But he also helps everybody see how silly it is to let their grumpiness go too far. He helps others "get over it" when they're frustrated. No matter how bad it gets, Grumpy Bear always comes back for more. He doesn't give up!

Don't even try to cheer me up!

All the Care Bears have a soft spot for Grumpy Bear. He gets along best with Tenderheart Bear and Friend Bear.

Even when you're feeling grumpy, feeling glad is just a mood away! Mad! Sad! Glad!

Today's my GRUMPY day

GOOD LUCK BEAR

Boy

Color: Green

Symbol: Four-leafed clover

Character Summary: Loaded with luck! "Today's my lucky day!"

Have you ever found a lucky four-leafed clover? If you're friends with Good Luck Bear, you've found your own personal lucky charm! Here's Good Luck Bear's secret to good luck: Always think good things will happen, and when they do—share them! He also has a way of making broken machines work—sometimes with just the snap of his fingers!

Good Luck Bear and Cheer Bear try to see who can be more upbeat! But sometimes, by accident, Good Luck Bear makes Grumpy Bear grumpier.

Today's my lucky day

Remember what Good Luck Bear says: "Practice makes lucky!"

Friend Bear

Girl

Color: Peach

Symbol: Two flowers

Character Summary
The perfect friend.
"Call me friend!"

You gotta have friends! And Friend Bear knows just how to make a friend and be a friend, through good times and bad. She likes to play and she's fun to be with! She's so caring and friendly she can charm almost anyone or anything—bears, plants, even clouds—to do what she wants. Friend Bear's a real chatterbox and sometimes she just can't stop talking!

My best bud is a bear!

Friend Bear is friendly with everyone, but her best buddy is Love-a-lot Bear.

Today and every day, Friend Bear says, "Make a friendship blossom!"

Friends R cool

LAUGH-A-LOT BEAR

Girl

Color: Orange

Symbol: Laughing star

Character Summary: Loves life! "Laughter's what I'm after!"

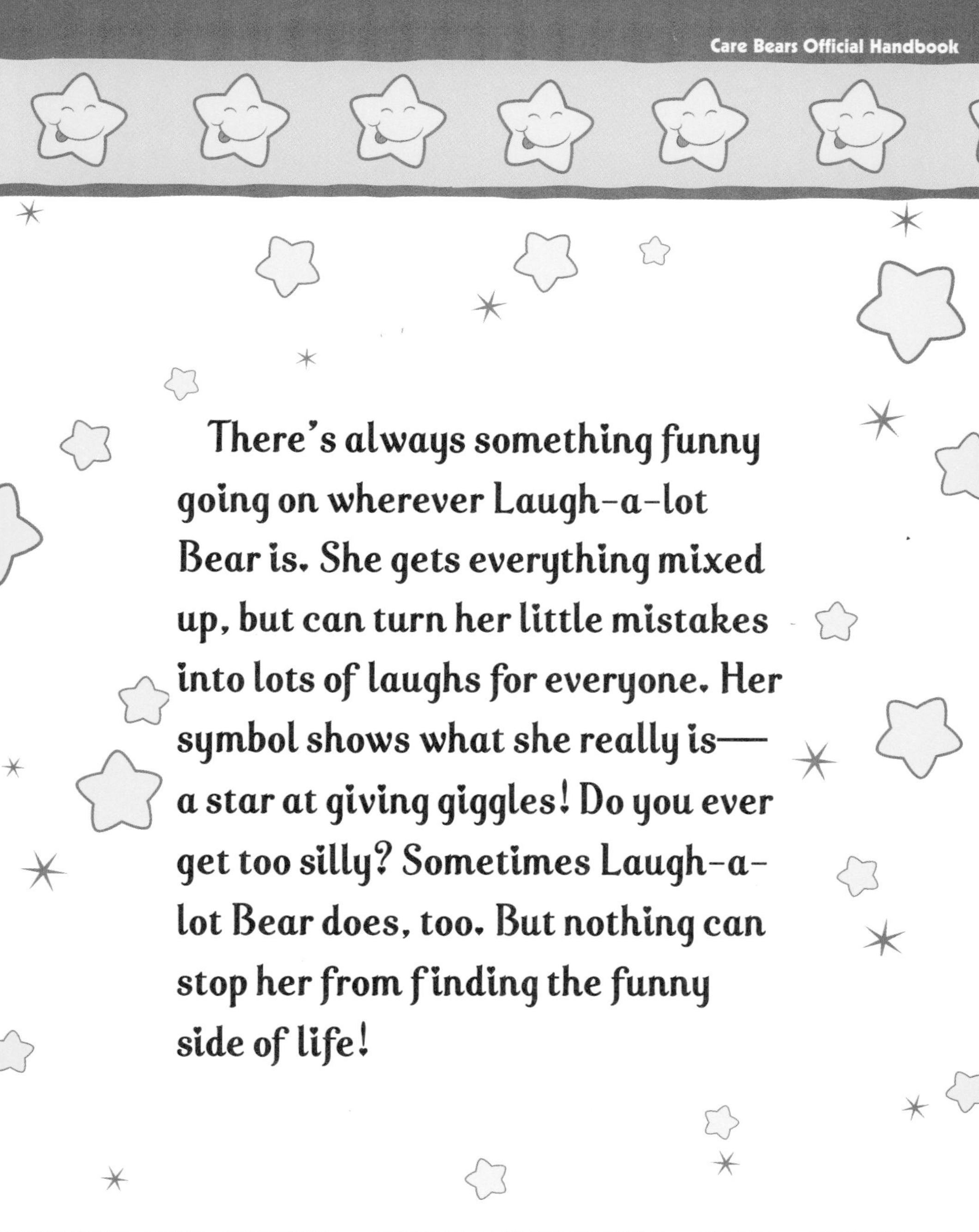

There's always something funny going on wherever Laugh-a-lot Bear is. She gets everything mixed up, but can turn her little mistakes into lots of laughs for everyone. Her symbol shows what she really is—a star at giving giggles! Do you ever get too silly? Sometimes Laugh-a-lot Bear does, too. But nothing can stop her from finding the funny side of life!

Keep laughing!

Laugh-a-lot Bear gives everyone the giggles, but she can make Grumpy Bear laugh so hard it hurts! Another special friend is Funshine Bear, but Laugh-a-lot Bear sometimes doesn't get Funshine Bear's jokes.

No matter what happens today,
"Get some giggles going!"

GIGGLE

Baby Hugs Bear

Girl

Color: Pink

Symbol: Smiling star with heart

Character Summary:

The tiniest, cutest, little girl Care Bear! What a cutie! Nobody could be sweeter than Baby Hugs Bear. She loves to give hugs to everyone. She's a curious little Care Bear, too, and gets into plenty of baby mischief. But all is forgiven when she gives one of her sweet baby hugs!

BABY TUGS BEAR

Boy

Color: Blue

Symbol: Star

Character Summary:

The tiniest, cutest, little boy Care Bear! He's a rough and tumble little guy, who can't wait to be a grown-up Care Bear! He copies everything the older Care Bears do. But no matter how much he tags along, he always tugs at your heart!

Star Buddies, Big and Small!

You'll find Star Buddies all over Care-a-lot. They are the Care Bears' very special friends. Some grow big enough to hold a swing for the Care Bears, while others stay as small as butterflies. Star Buddies love to tag along and follow the Care Bears wherever they go. They can be helpful, too!

Why Star Buddies Are Nice to Have Around—Reason #1

If you live in the clouds, Star Buddies are the perfect playmates.

Why Star Buddies Are Nice to Have Around—Reason #2

Star Buddies can help make wishes come true.(But sometimes you'll wish you wished for something different!)

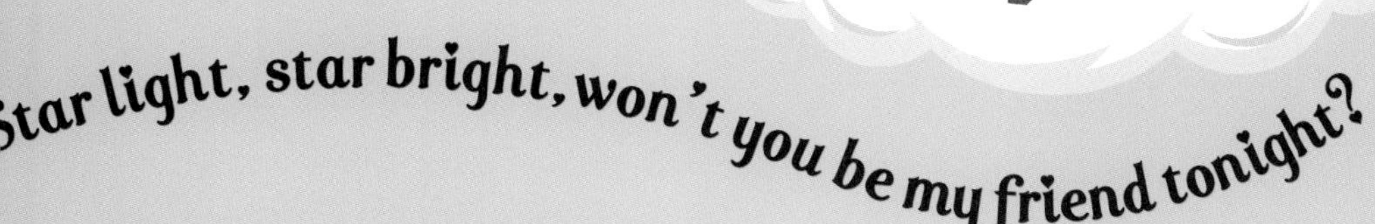

Star light, star bright, won't you be my friend tonight?

Why Star Buddies Are Nice to Have Around—Reason #3
Star Buddies love to deliver messages, and they're faster than e-mail!

Why Star Buddies Are Nice to Have Around—Reason #4
They'll do anything to make you laugh!

Why Star Buddies Are Nice to Have Around—Reason #5

Star Buddies help bring sweet dreams!

Why Star Buddies Are Nice to Have Around—Reason #6

It's simple—Star Buddies are cool!

Boy

Color: Purple

Symbol: Heart and stocking cap

Character Summary: The perfect host

Cozy Heart Penguin loves to throw parties! He always makes his friends feel right at home. And he helps them forget their worries, especially when they're in a new place or trying something for the first time. All the Care Bear Cousins come to him when they're not sure about their manners. From please to thank you, Cozy Heart Penguin always knows the right thing to say and the right way to act.

PROUD HEART CAT

Girl

Color: Aqua

Symbol: Star with heart center

Character Summary: Purrrrrrrfectionist!

Proud Heart Cat always gives her very best in everything she does. And even better, she helps others do their best, too. The other Care Bear Cousins love to kid her about her funny little cat-habits. For instance, she's super-clean and will do whatever it takes to not get dirty! And every hair on her head has to be perfect before she'll leave the house. But Proud Heart Cat always reminds her friends how important it is to try to do our best!

LOYAL HEART DOG

Boy

Color: Blue

Symbol: Heart medal

Character Summary:
Loyal friend

Need a true-blue friend? Loyal Heart Dog is just that. His kind of loyalty deserves a medal, and that's why he wears one for his tummy-symbol!

PLAYFUL HEART MONKEY

Boy

Color: Gold

Symbol: Heart balloon and party favors

Character Summary: Master of monkey business!

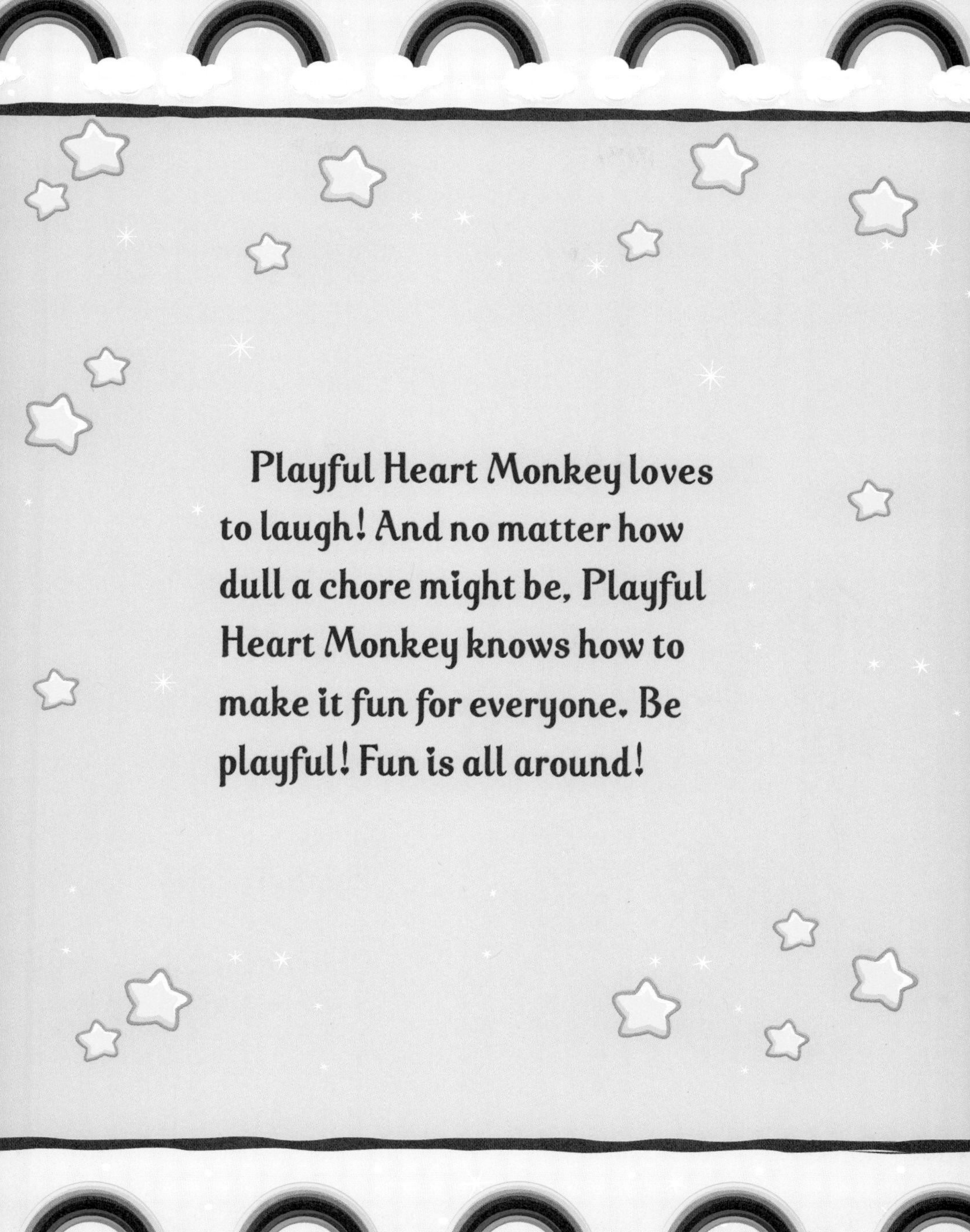

Playful Heart Monkey loves to laugh! And no matter how dull a chore might be, Playful Heart Monkey knows how to make it fun for everyone. Be playful! Fun is all around!

GENTLE HEART LAMB

Girl

Color: Mint green

Symbol: Pillow heart

Character Summary: Soft-hearted as a pillow

Gentle Heart Lamb is the most trusting and kind of all the Care Bear Cousins. She always knows just what to say when someone's feeling sad and she's always ready to help, no matter what, by sharing her love, kindness, and encouragement.

BRIGHT HEART RACCOON

Boy

Color: Lavender

Symbol: Glowing heart lightbulb

Character Summary: The Care Bear Cousin with the brightest ideas and the brightest smile!

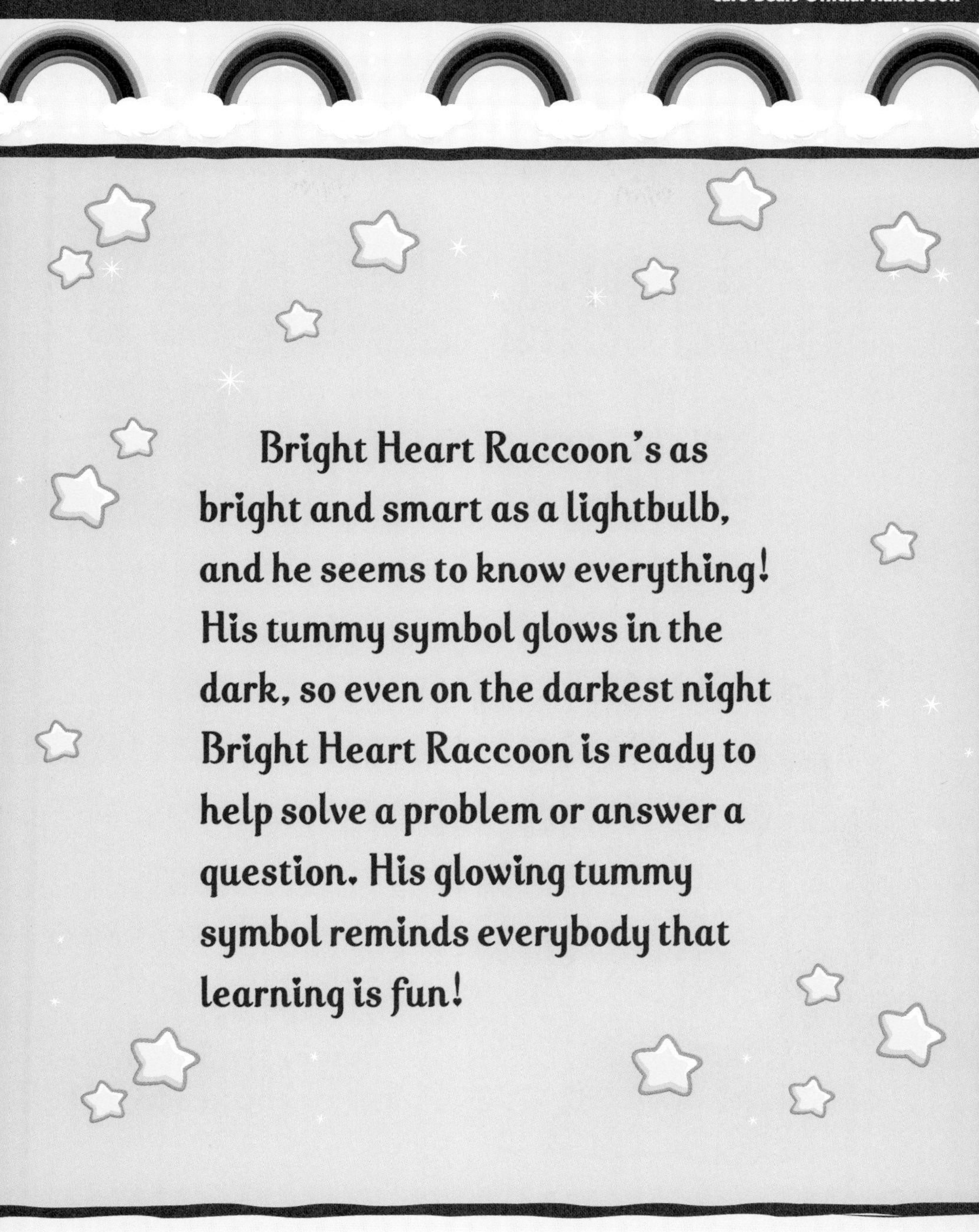

Bright Heart Raccoon's as bright and smart as a lightbulb, and he seems to know everything! His tummy symbol glows in the dark, so even on the darkest night Bright Heart Raccoon is ready to help solve a problem or answer a question. His glowing tummy symbol reminds everybody that learning is fun!

LOTSA HEART ELEPHANT

Girl

Color: Pink

Symbol: Exercise weight with heart

Character Summary: Full of encouragement!

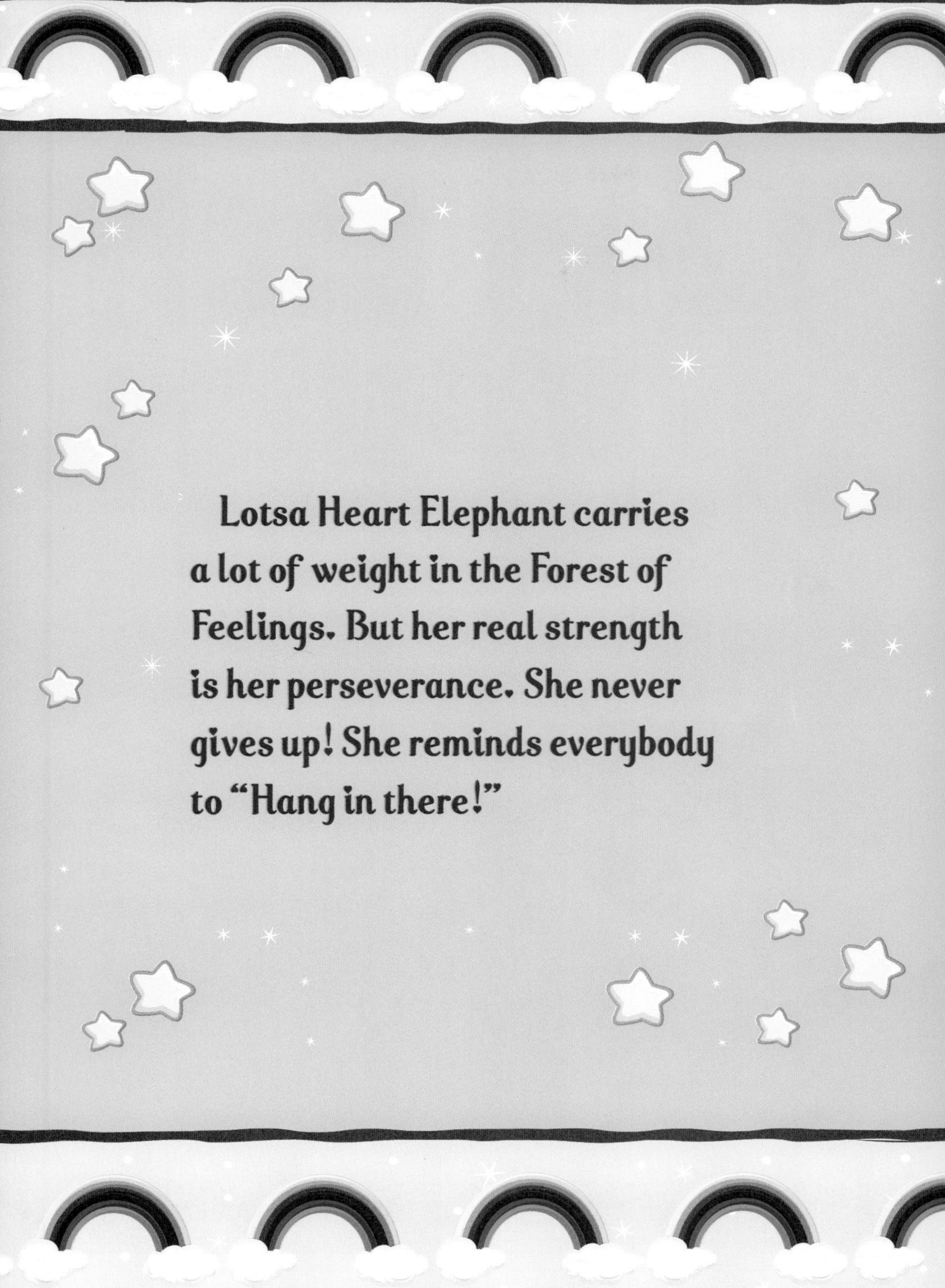

Lotsa Heart Elephant carries a lot of weight in the Forest of Feelings. But her real strength is her perseverance. She never gives up! She reminds everybody to "Hang in there!"

SWIFT HEART RABBIT

Girl

Color: Blue

Symbol: Heart with wings

Character Summary:
Fastest feelings in the forest!

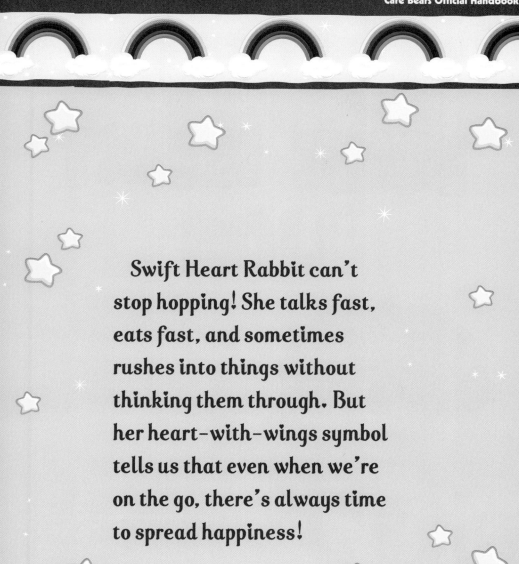

Swift Heart Rabbit can't stop hopping! She talks fast, eats fast, and sometimes rushes into things without thinking them through. But her heart-with-wings symbol tells us that even when we're on the go, there's always time to spread happiness!

BRAVE HEART LiON

Boy

Color: Orange

Symbol: Heart with crown

Character Summary: Caring leader

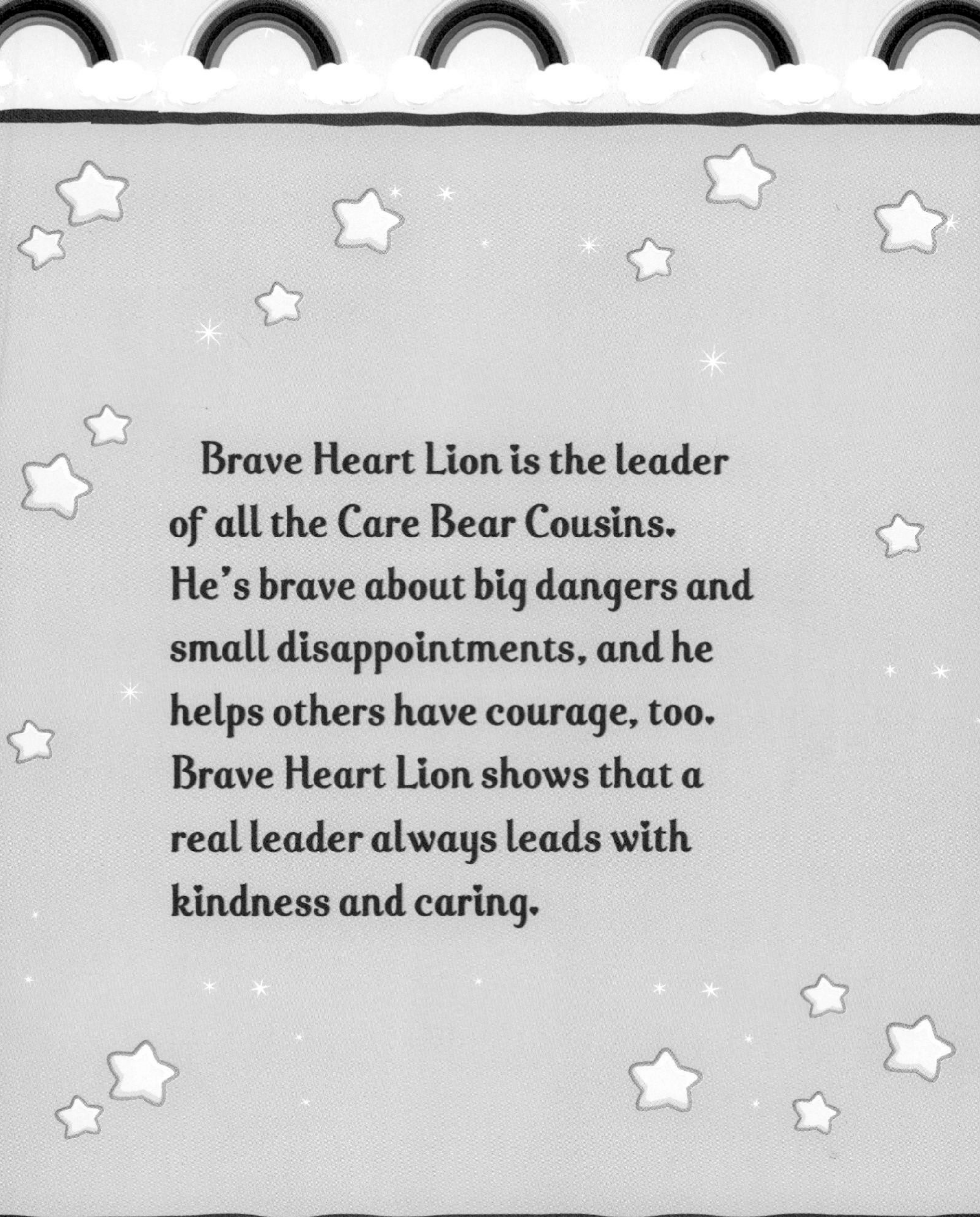

Brave Heart Lion is the leader of all the Care Bear Cousins. He's brave about big dangers and small disappointments, and he helps others have courage, too. Brave Heart Lion shows that a real leader always leads with kindness and caring.

Thanks for visiting
Care-a-lot!